JOAN W. BLOS

O·L·D H·E·N·R·Y

ILLUSTRATED BY

STEPHEN GAMMELL

WILLIAM MORROW & CO., INC. / NEW YORK

The story begins when a stranger appears
and moves into a house that was vacant for years.

No one thought he meant to stay;
the house was drafty, dark and gray,
and more than seven years had passed
since anyone had lived there last.

HOUSE
FOR
RENT

He meant to stay.

He had no doubt.
It suited him from inside out,
and in its vast and dusty spaces
all the things he had
found places.

That Henry!

The neighbors watched him moving in
and promised each other he'd soon begin
to fix things up a bit.

He did not think of it.

With money enough to pay the rent,
his books, birds, and cooking pots,
he was content
and never did notice (or else didn't care)
that people whispered everywhere:
                "That place
                is a disgrace."

"At least," they remarked, "you would think that he could show a little respect for the neighborhood."

"That place is a disgrace."

At last they decided to form a committee
and went to him saying, "We are proud of our city.
If you'd only help out, think how good it would look—"
"Excuse me." He bowed,
and went back to his book.

That Henry.

Then they fined him fines. They threatened jail.
They wrote him long letters and sent them by mail:
"Dear Henry…"

Still the hollyhocks wilted, unwatered, unkept;
the gatepost stayed crooked, the walk stayed unswept.
And things went on as they'd begun,
and he angered his neighbors, one by one.

"Can't we *make* him sweep his walks?"
"No, there's nothing we can do—
You nasty Polly! Shoo, bird, shoo!"

"So unfriendly!"

"Never talks!"

On a day in November they sought the advice
of the mayor, who suggested being nice.

"Being *nice?*"

"Please,

try it twice."

But when two of the ladies baked him a pie,
he said, "I'm not hungry. No, thank you. Good-bye."

And when three of the men said they'd shovel his snow,
he quickly said: "No!"

"We told you so!"

Now Henry, too, had had his fill.
That night he grumbled, "I never *will*
live like the rest of them, neat and the same.
I am sorry I came."

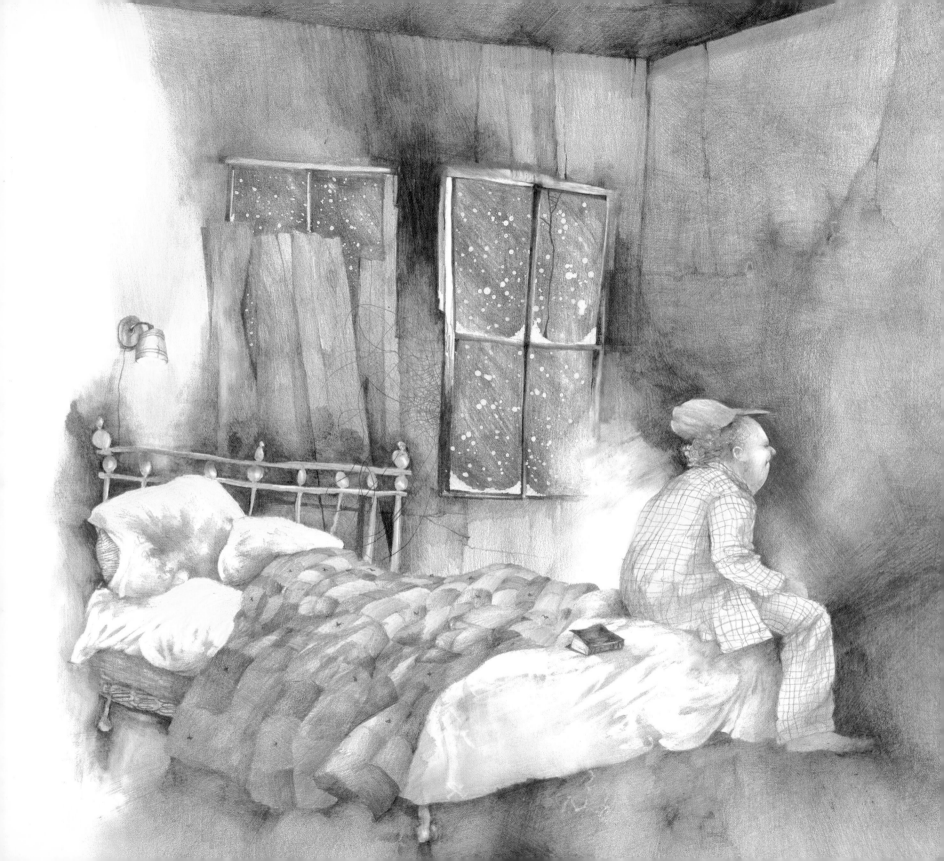

Then he packed some things in shopping bags
and tied the rest in three old rags.
He didn't make plans, he just left a short note, a
hastily written: G o n e   t o   D a k o t a

He taped it to the big front door.

And no one lived there

anymore.

His day lilies bloomed; his phlox grew tall.

They picked his apples in the fall.
They picked his apples and now and then
someone would ask, "Remember when…?
Remember when…?
Remember when…?"

Later still, in winter's snow,
they asked one another, "Where did he go?"
"Will he come again?"

"His house looks so empty, so dark in the night."
"And having him gone doesn't make us more right."
That Henry.

"Maybe, some other time, we'd get along
not thinking that somebody *has* to be wrong."
"And we don't have to make such a terrible fuss
because everyone isn't exactly like us."

Meanwhile, Old Henry, to his great surprise,
was missing the neighbors who'd brought him the pies.
In spite of their nagging, he really did care
for them and their street. So he wrote to the mayor:

Dear Mr. Mayor,

   I am finding it hard
to be far from my house
and my tree and my yard.

   If I mended the gate,
and I shoveled the snow,
would they not scold my birds?
Could I let my grass grow?

   Please write and tell me
the answers so then we
can all get together.

                    Sincerely yours,
                        Henry

Printed in Hong Kong.
3   4   5   6   7   8   9   10

Library of Congress Cataloging-in-Publication Data
Blos, Joan W.
Old Henry.
Summary: Henry's neighbors are scandalized that
he ignores them and lets his property get run down,
until they drive him away and find themselves
missing him.
[1. Neighborliness—Fiction. 2. Stories in
rhyme] I. Gammell, Stephen, ill. II. Title.
PZ8.3.B598401   1987   [E]   86-21745
ISBN 0-688-06399-3
ISBN 0-688-06400-0 (lib. bdg.)